THE CHANGE

Niall Twohig

Published by
Charybdis Press
www.charybdispress.com

This story is a work fiction. Any characters resembling actual persons living or dead is entirely coincidental.

Layout, Artwork & Design: Jason Blasso

ISBN 978-1-957399-32-4

For ma,
to give in words
what is hard to give in life

And these children that you spit on
As they try to change their worlds
Are immune to your consultations
They're quite aware of what they're goin' through
Ch-ch-ch-ch-changes
Turn and face the strange

David Bowie

The scars on our children's faces
will look for you.
Our children's amputated legs
will run after you.

Mosab Abu Toha

Contents

THE CHANGE

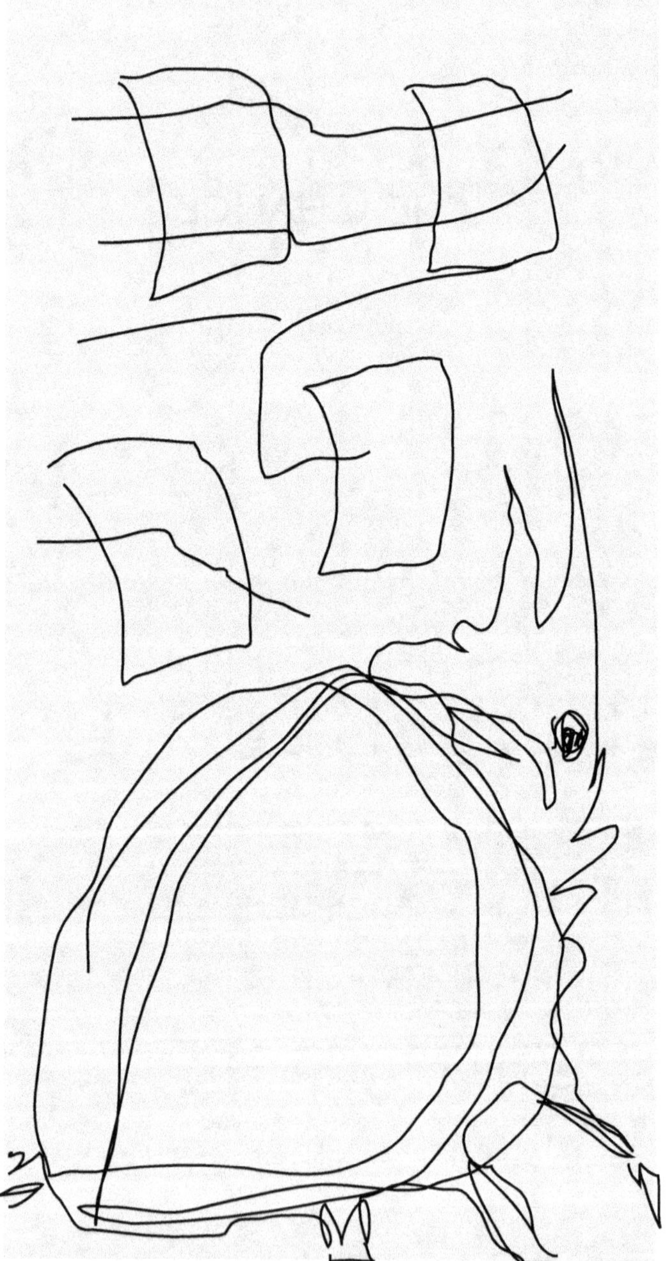

I. Metamorphosis

On the night the encampment was raided, N found himself transformed into a dung beetle. He wasn't at the encampment when the change occurred. Other commitments kept him home.

But he was "there in spirit." That's what he had told himself, and what he texted a friend who was there, but now that was an alien thought fading to pure insectile movement.

So, he moved. He heaved himself to his desk and clawed the stack of student essays. Maybe he would have marked them had he fingers to leaf pages, to hold pen, to write notes. Maybe he would have read them had he eyes to focus on lines and words rather than what he saw now: a kaleidoscopic explosion of words. Had he been human, maybe he would have done his work. Maybe.

Or maybe not. His insect mind still held the faint outline of his last human rumination:

I can't do this.

He knew then, before the change, that each paper he graded took him over the picket line. His union had called the work stoppage in solidarity with the encampment. This meant no teaching or grading. Yet his commitment to his students proved stronger than the union's call.

Commitment. Had it been that? Or had he used his students, used the safe cloister of his work, to avoid facing the fear of being at the encampment in body rather than spirit?

A layer lower still, nestled under that questionable commitment, was a deeper rationalization. The thought that he had given something *more* with his words. He had taken up his pen, like an insurgent's rifle, aimed first at the administration and then widening his scope to UC San Diego as a whole. Already fifty signatures. Already published in the student newspapers. Hadn't writing earned him a right not to be there?

Had he been human, this mess of thoughts would have led to an impasse. Had he been human, he would have sat here, at his desk, clawing dumbly at the papers in this same futile way.

But he was no longer human with ten fingers, simple eyes, a mind churning in on itself as it strains, impossibly, to rationalize the convictions of the heart.

Only embers of that mind remained and these were overshadowed by a simpler impulse: to roll that little object he once called "ballpoint pen" over the thing called "paper." He knew this process, rolling ballpoint over surface, once led to food. When his action proved futile — when the ballpoint pen could not be clutched or rolled, when no food appeared — the impulse was replaced by new attempts at gratifying deeply rooted needs.

* * *

The change seemed to occur all at once but, in truth, it had been growing for decades. N felt the first stirrings during the shock and awe of Iraq and then again, decades later, when he taught an Iraqi student who described childhood games where she and her brothers raced to the roof to collect spent bullet casings.

He doubled over after hearing that story, a wave of nausea overwhelming him, as cells died and were reborn, tentacled and chitinous, if one had the lens to see. That feeling intensified over the last ten months of bombing abroad and campus unrest at home. After what felt like a panic attack, he looked closely at his skin. Each pore seemed a miniature black head that, with a little pressure, might erupt.

The pressure came while scrolling social media. His feed showed a flashback of N with his ma, smiling in the sun, on the boardwalk washed away by Superstorm Sandy (scroll) another shrouded baby surrounded by wailing men and women (scroll) a silly ginger cat mistiming his leap (scroll) the encampment surrounded by riot police and several protestors, braver than he, clubbed and arrested.

The juxtaposition of the media, culminating in the clean

circle of a zip tie around wrists, was the final catalyst that allowed the hard black shell to tear through N's dried skin leaving behind a hollow molting of the man he had become.

He paused before the skin as he once paused before an old suit he loved but that no longer fit. In that old life, he hesitated before the suit but ultimately left it in the alley where old things became new for the unhoused.

Without thought, N followed that old pattern. He heaved his armored body around till his rhino-like horn aligned with fallen flesh, probed tibial teeth till they caught, agitated the leg until the bag of his former self flapped up and caught around his horn. Skin draped like a flag, he trudged through the side door and back gate, entered the alley, and unceremoniously tossed the remnant atop an abandoned sofa. The sweeping motion carried the weight of his horn, and subsequently his whole hulking body, to a reverse course. He had never moved with such precision, such terrifyingly unsentimental grace.

II. No Words

The day after the encampment was raided, N's students came to class despite Chancellor K's message urging them to stay home. Some came because they were in shock and wanted space to talk or listen. Others came because they hadn't read the chancellor's message and didn't know of the beatings and arrests.

N stood silently in his usual spot at the front of the room. His students waited for him to speak but, for the first time, he didn't have words or, for that matter, the physiology to articulate recognizable sounds.

So, they stared into his silent onyx exoskeleton until it became a dark mirror. Unable to take their own silent reflection, a few spoke.

— What the fuck was that! I don't understand.

— What was what?

— The police beat the shit out of the protestors.

— My friend got pepper sprayed.

— You should see the huge bruise on my roommate's ribs!

— Seriously? I was working in the CS dungeon all nite. I had no idea.

— Did the protestors do something wrong?

— I don't think so.

— We didn't do anything. We were asleep. They woke us with a loud siren. They came like robots, with dead eyes. We formed lines, held together arm in arm. Then they came harder. Pushed us. Herded us toward the library. One came at me and my friend. He clubbed her in the face. I ran. I didn't know where. I just ran and cried. I wanted to stop. What kept me going were the images of Rafah, images of my people running. They ran, like I was running, but I didn't have to step over dead bodies. They did. That got me home.

Silence, then a student stirs and erupts at her peers.

— How the fuck can you be silent! How the fuck can you be silent! We help make the bombs here. Right here. At this university. And you do nothing. You sit there. Silent! And when we stand up, when we say enough is enough, when we march peacefully, they beat the shit out of us. And you sit there silent! How!

A primal howl. It causes some to redden and shift in their seats. N stirs too, an instinctive pull toward the chitin he feels under this student's skin. He slowly points his horn toward her and lurches closer to show he'll aid her if she is threatened.

Those words, paired with N's subtle shift, causes a student to react.

— I didn't do anything wrong. I've busted my ass to be here. I'm silent because I've got shit to do. Anyway, the protestors have said and done nasty shit. I don't feel comfortable with them camped out there.

— Did you see them do bad stuff? I mean, I walked by and I saw folks dancing and praying. At one point, Jewish students passed out plates of watermelon.

— I saw videos online from here, from places around the country. Antisemitic shit. My mom told me protestors would be happy to see me dead.

— My folks say the same. But my roommate's been at the encampment. He's Muslim. He doesn't want me dead. He's a good dude. Look. Here's a pic of what they did to him.

He shows the photo of an ugly poppy bruise streaked across a brown torso.

Silence again as they wait for their professor to relieve the tension. Nothing. Only that cold dark stare that reflects the tension to infinity as if they are in a hall of mirrors. Trapped in that hall, their minds look to the outer reaches to see if something is staring back and laughing at this fraught conversation, laughing at the violence that inspired it. Or perhaps their minds find something other than a devil in this tension stretched to a silent infinity. Perhaps they find—

— Professor, um, a question: When will get our essays back?

With that, the students are pulled back, back from the hall of mirrors to the classroom. They walk into the midday sun eclipsed now by distant traumas closer to home. So close for some that they feel the darkness under their skin, waiting to erupt.

NO MORE
Rest through Peace

III. Silence Equals Death

N's body knew it had to be at an appointed place at an appointed time. The scent of coffee drew him to the Mandeville cart where his boss, the Director of English, waited for him smiling warmly despite the marked tension on his face.

N scanned the surroundings, seeking the outward source of the creature's tension. All seemed calm even the jagged and vibrant graffiti written on canvases approved by the administration. Staring into those rectangles, N saw a palimpsest of symbols, indignance brushed into some, and thin white coating after thin white coating that hid away the layered rage.

When the director spoke, N felt his voice carrying more symbols all contained within an invisible frame much like those canvases.

Look, N, I wanted to grab coffee because I'm worried about you. You've changed these last few months.

You're short with me and with colleagues who are not quick to take sides. You've been using "genocide" in your classes.

You're at rallies chanting along to slogans that, honestly, make me feel uncomfortable.

This isn't the N that I know. You're a listener, not a yeller. You open discussion rather than shutting it down.

I'm trying to understand what has changed. Really. Help me to understand.

Then, there's the statement you wrote. I know you want me to sign. Here's the thing. I agree with much of what you wrote, especially the part where you call out the administration for demonizing the protestors. That's their right. Free speech.

But you lost me when you turn to the bigger issue. I just don't think the situation is as simple as you write: life against death, liberation against systemic oppression, silence equaling death.

And there's the tone of the piece. Angry.

The N I know wouldn't write like that. He'd make room for different sides. He'd invite everyone into the conversation. He'd use his words to build bridges.

What you wrote isn't that. So, I'm not on board.

Funny. That's what it feels like. You and others boarded a bus to a place I'm not ready to go. I know what you might think. I'm on the wrong side of history for not boarding. Maybe. But I am where I am.

I hope you can understand, N. Anyway, no need to respond now. We'll circle back when things cool down. Let me get you a coffee.

The old N, dissolving now like an ingested tablet, knew this creature well. They had labored together, had a bond. But new sensory organs focused on the present not the past. Reading the creature's tone and body language, N knew it posed no immediate threat. But something set off a pulse that ran from antennae, down his segmented belly, back up to his mandibles.

It was the surface tension around the creature's smile. It put N on the defensive. He saw the tension stemming from a deep unexplored fear, fear coated in a thick but fragile layer of kindness and passivity. This egg was harvested for something out there, something dangerous: an apex predator that won its prize by remaining unseen and unspoken by its prey. Here was Its caviar, the egg It relished most.

Sensing this looming threat, N acted instinctively.

Snapping forward, he plunged his horn into the creature's heart as mandibles gyrated through its frightened meat. N felt the tension break, saw its fear exposed, felt cellular relief become a bliss elusive in life. The old N, a shadow now, knew he would keep his friend safe inside as he moved closer to the Thing hunting at the peripheries of the human eye. Even shadows seek consolation, it seems.

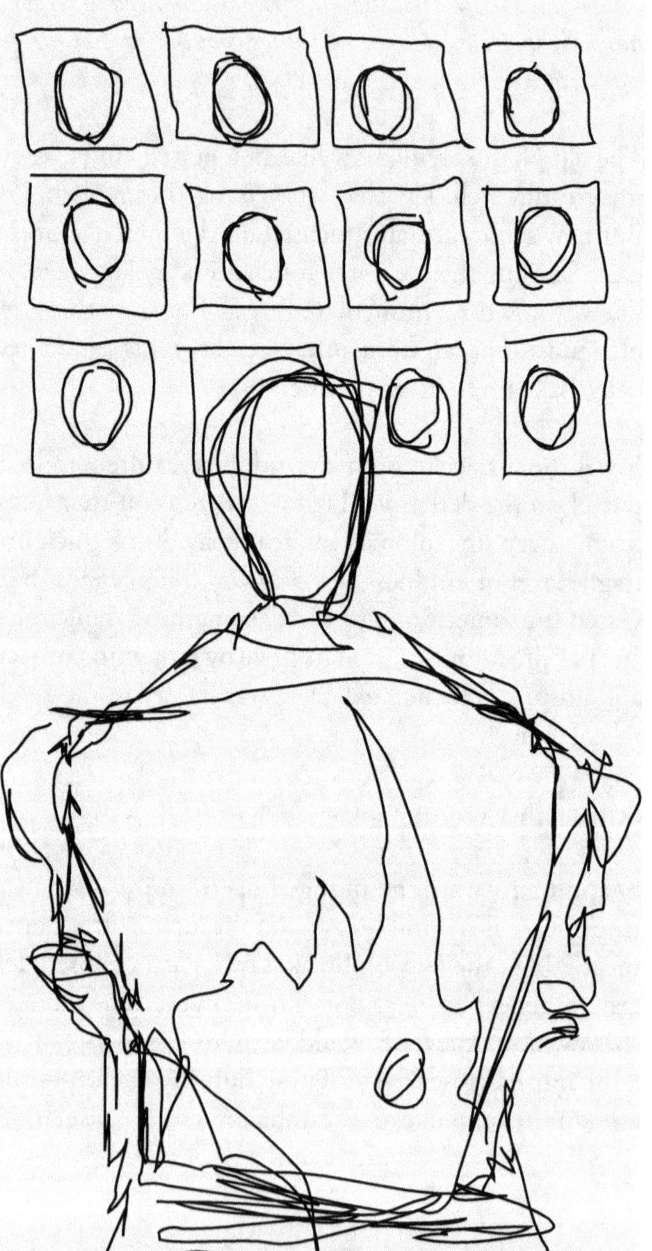

IV. Haunted House

It was a wet and stormy night in La Jolla, not so uncharacteristic given the Anthropocenic changes making this dry land blossom lush as a desert flower before the killing heat.

The dark mass of N slithered Westward, through the torrent, rivulets giving him an undulating effect, as if a giant swell of worms had become one.

What drew N to the coast was a beacon. From the university, he had seen a pillar of light through the clouds and now, as he made his way up La Jolla Farms Road, he saw its point of emanation.

The Audrey Geisel house was lit from underneath, sacred land sent up a spotlight into the drenched air. Hovering in that beam of light was a dark mark, as when a sticker is pressed to flashlight glass.

That house was a darkness. What lived here, in life, remained in death.

Coming to its outer gate, N smelled pride, and below

that fresh smell, the aged aroma of grief buried alongside an intricate web of being that the old N would have no adequate words to describe. The closest description he could have given would be to say that what lay buried resembled a dream-catcher that smelled of sage and sand, blood and tobacco.

Looking in, N saw the tribesmen and women dancing around the house. Most human eyes would not see them but, if the Kumeyaay elders were there, they would have sensed their ancestors moving in this ghost dance.

Others, inside the house, saw the dancers too. Their seven gossamer faces were framed in the bay window. They looked out at the dance in terror, holding their translucent fingers to the glass as if to firm it up.

As N broke through the gate, the ghost dancers intensified their pace. Somewhere, deep below the surface, their twenty-nine pulverized hearts became a single drum beat timed to the last beats of N's human heart and the beginnings of the one in his gut.

Seeing the beast at their door, the chancellors of old opened their mouths in a silent scream heard by no one, not even themselves.

* * *

In calm orange chandelier light, Chancellor K sat on a plush sofa staring into the glowing screen that held other shiny faces looking in from rooms with blurred or artificial backgrounds. Each person on the video call focused on the tiny box that held their own face.

Damage control. That's what these faces were at, though their mouths would never call it that. They had many bullet points to talk through. But within the penumbra of those points were two simple questions they would never say aloud: How do we keep our image clean? How do we get this machine running at full throttle?

They didn't make it far in their agenda. The conversation stopped dead when a vice chancellor saw a dark figure standing in the background the chancellor forgot to blur.

— *Um, sir. I think there's something in your room.*

— *What's that?*

— *There's something there. It just moved behind your curtains. There it goes again.*

Seeing the movement on screen, the chancellor's first dumb instinct was to snap his laptop shut, as if to hide some embarrassing decoration, as if the background itself was a blemish on his face.

But then, it sunk in: the reality of what was said and what he had seen on screen. He turned, breathless, to face the thing behind the curtains.

— *Who are you? How did you get in here? Get out!*

He puffed himself up like John Wayne, unholstering his

bravado that, for a moment, had almost slipped away with fright.

N read the chancellor's changing chemistry. The fear, there for a moment, was covered now by a rush of emotion that came on like a cavalry encircling the fear and stomping it out of existence. N did not need such metaphors to understand that the bravado, the willpower that followed, was familiar to this desecrated land. He could feel the land's heart beat faster and harder in his gut.

Still veiled by the curtain, N lurched forward and, as he did, his horn slid across the veil till it tore through, showing the sharp point.

The curved horn made the chancellor think of the functions he had graphed as an engineer. He thought of that point in certain curves where, after reaching their zenith, slope downward. The critical point.

Is this mine?

The thought, there for a fraction of a second, was pushed out of his mind by a sound.

It came from below his feet. Pounding. With each beat, the sound rose to the surface till it was there, in the room, rattling through his bones. Pounding. As if given permission by the sound, N tore through the curtain showing the chancellor the full onyx of his being. Pounding. The chancellor was frozen. He saw his face reflected. In that instant, he thought, not of the kingdom he had built, but of the time lost with loved ones while building. Pounding. He thought, not of the things he had engineered, but of the lives his engineering had taken. Pounding. In the blackness, the haggard face of a man trying to reach his dying father, a face that, when turned to ones and zeroes, set off alarms that slowed his passage through barbed wire gates. Pounding. In the blackness the face of a child on the other end of a weaponized drone who, in one click, would be turned to "bug splat" on far off screens.

Seeing those faces sent a chill down the chancellor's spine. No ordinary chill, for in that moment he turned a ghastly and permanent white, as pale as the ghosts that skulked in the corners of the room, terrified of what stalked without and within.

The chancellor stared into his death mask reflected in the black mirror. Transfixed, he mouthed words he associated, less with a sacred text than with a scientist.

> *We have become Death*
> *destroyer of worlds.*

The "we" didn't belong, he knew, but it made sense given how the great death force, wielded once by mighty men, had dispersed outward, across a vast machine, to which he and his class of men were functional parts. Dispersed outward until its million little mushroom clouds could no longer be seen, at least not for those who lived far beyond the thousand-foot blast radiuses. Try as they might to show the world their technological wonders, these functionaries can't hide the rot of their work. It comes for them.

That rot. The chancellor could smell it around him. No. *In* and *on* him. He was rotting, like the house, like all the things he and men had made, only faster.

I could die right now, he thought with a weird sense of relief as gravity tempted him to the ground.

What held him up was a memory from childhood. He saw himself a boy in Bombay turning the page of the *Bhagavad Gita* comic to see the blue god standing with a man gone soft, a pathetic man who tried to flee the war to be fought in his name. The boy flipped the page to see the man accept his greatness. And then: the two-page spread of the cosmic carnage his armies wrought.

There is no stepping away from one's dharma.

He knew who he was: Chancellor K. He stood proud, turned, and ran for the safe room where, by the grace of God, he would live to fight another day.

N felt the creature's chemical bravado return, stronger now because of that electrochemical image. N saw the image too, felt its alchemy push away the creature's fear and propel his legs toward flight. Gone was the drumbeat pounding in his gut. It quieted, leaving only the pure motion of the hunt.

The white ghosts cowered as N gave chase, but their

pride was restored as their living brother made it to his locked box.

Within that box, the chancellor heard the pounding and scraping against the titanium door. Security cameras flickered on and closed-circuit showed N's wild motion which, on the screen, brought to mind spiders that seem to disappear as they leap from point to point. Seeing this, the chancellor's terror turned to awe. *A true force of nature!* He knew who he had to call. Yes, the riot police. But also, a man with a mind to harness this brute.

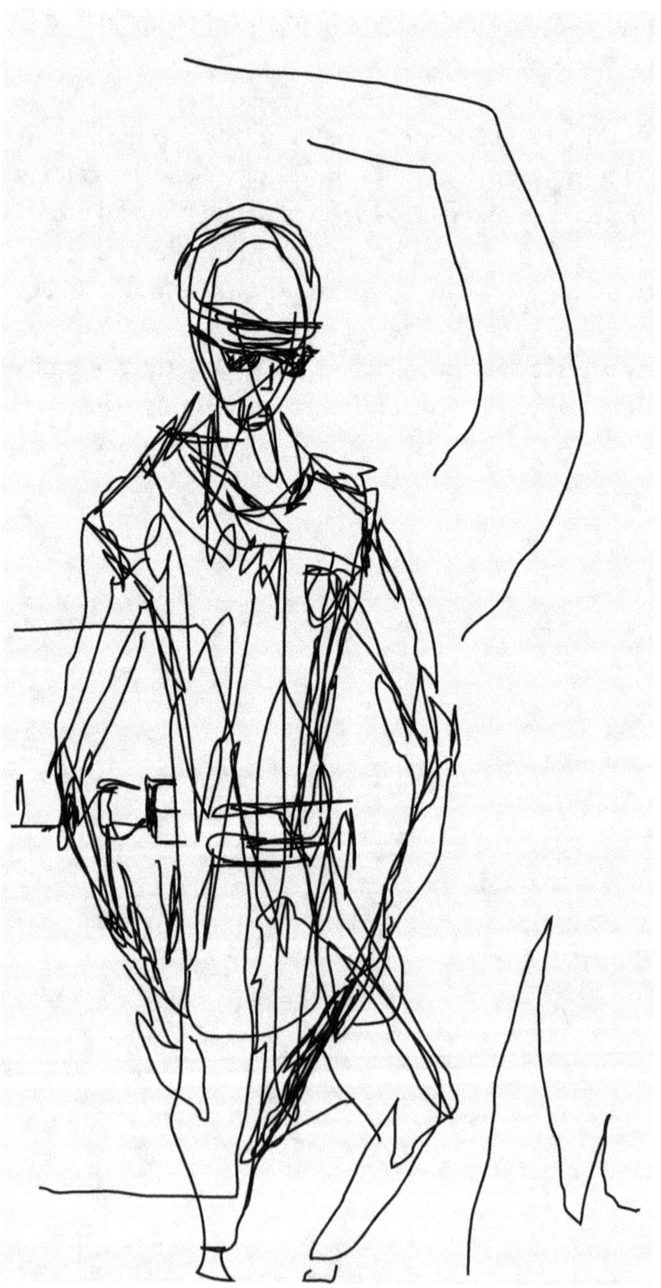

V. Break Things Better

N saw the hollow in the riot police as they came at him. A vacant spot, like that on a dying tree, where only desperate creatures crawl in winter. He saw that hollow filled by the Thing in the shadows. Possessed, they became Its fingers wrapped in a Kevlar gloves, holding polycarbonate shields, gripping metal billy clubs. N knew it would be death to resist Its hand. So, he yielded, crouching his hulking mass to the floor. And still they beat his fleshy underside. He yielded. And still, they tased him. He yielded. And still they fired sonic shockwaves to boil his blood.

Once N was shackled, the police made room for a man who N, even in his brokenness, could feel was closer to the Thing.

His name was Dr. Syme. Pull up his X account and you'd see the tags pathfinder, entrepreneur, disruptor. Pull up his department website and you'd find his elevator pitch, "Gerhard Syme breaks ground at the interstices of neuroscience, nanotech, AI and security."

Despite such lofty descriptions, Syme was mostly nondescript. Skinny jeans, a grey sweatshirt, old school Reeboks. His only accessory were sunglasses worn at all times, not as a fashion statement, but as a technological third eye. They read all available data points, relayed them to the cloud and processed them through AI algorithms, to instantaneously tell Syme exactly what he saw. And what he saw, laid out and broken, made him giddy.

Curious. Curious. Some change has come upon this man. That's clear to those with eyes to see. But he can be fixed. We have just the tech, just the tech. And he deserves that much. After all, he's a great asset to this university: an award-winning teacher. A promising writer. Yes yes. It appears he had something to do with that nasty business with the English director. I'm not condoning what may have happened. No no. But you don't need a bigger mess on your hands. So, let's scrub that story. And I'll give you a better one that adds to the prestige of this place, that ensures your diamond legacy!

* * *

Trailing behind a police escort, Syme's research team wheeled N on a gurney through an empty Revelle Plaza. A message from Syme, relayed through their glasses, ordered them to pause until the path was clear.

They stopped in front of the May 1970 Peace Memorial. Its light exploded in N's eyes. Each fixture became a cross of light that connected to the next creating a crazy hopscotch pattern. The more N fixated, the more labyrinthine the pattern became.

Afraid of getting lost in that light, N pushed his awareness beyond that constellation, south to Galbraith Hall. There, leaning on the railing, stood a wizened professor with tussled white hair and wooden pipe in his mouth. He cooly moved match to pipe, illuminating piercing eyes. Those eyes, they knew the forces that make some men into saints and most others into monsters.

The violence is not with you.

As he said it, he melted into air. The last vespers of his pipe smoke floated into the now cloudless sky, reaching for stars as we reach, hopeful despite our limits.

Getting the "all clear" from Syme, the team wheeled N around, violently, shifting his body toward the North where, at the corner of the water fountain, he saw the burning man, not as he died, but as he remained outside of history. In a lotus posture.

The man mouthed names. As he did so, a fiery tongue licked up from his body to the air where it wrote a name in flame that burned seamlessly into the next.

Aaron Bushnell Sha'ban al-Dalou
Farah al-Dalou Matthew Nelson

The silent fire-kissed list would eventually begin anew only longer next time, an infinite loop, like mala or a prayer wheel, that grew in its turning. That wheel of fire turned as the man looked to N with eyes full of tears despite the fiery halo engulfing him. N felt the gaze penetrate his dented hide. It warmed his cold blood. Had he tear ducts, N would have cried. In their absence, his whole body sobbed.

As the gurney reached the plaza's north side, N felt another presence looking down from Urey Hall. Ghosts of an older occupation. They bore witness to this crime while their living descendants slept. They called to others, more shades, who streamed into the plaza holding signs that read No to War, Give Peace a Chance, End Apartheid, and Not in Our Name. These ghosts reached for N, tried to free him, settled on singing a freedom song that comforted the insect as he was wheeled to death.

Un pueblo unido jamas será vencido.

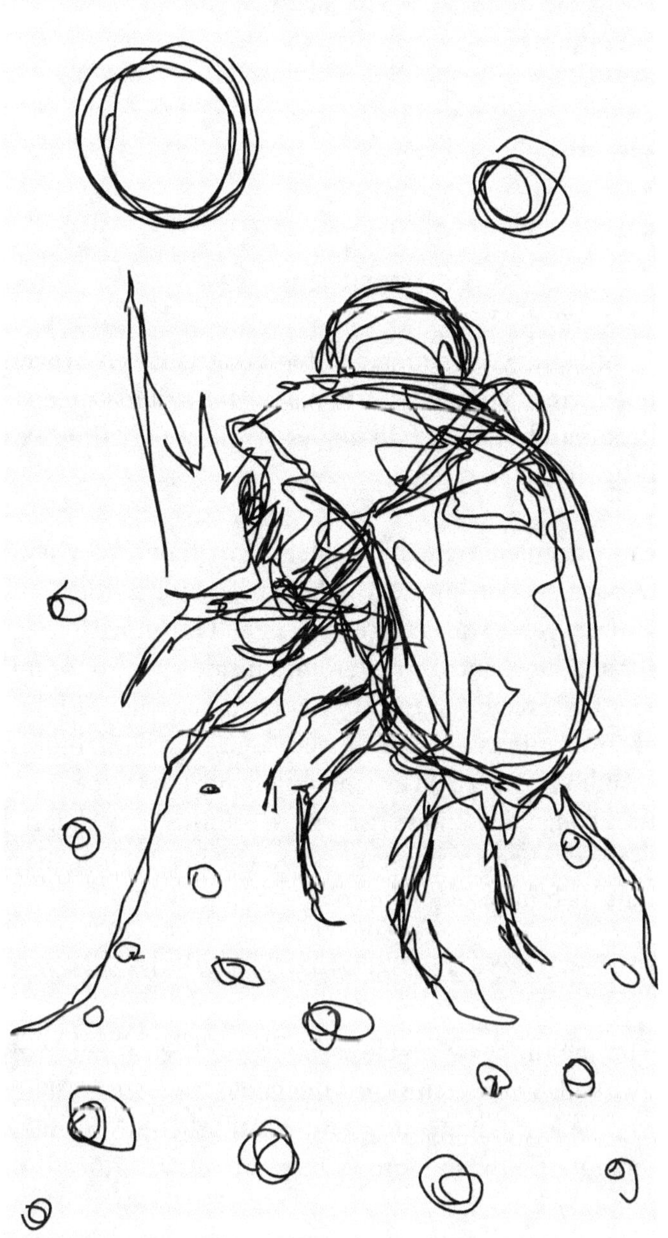

Interlude. Ma

Chained in cold storage, N looks squashed. A broken outer wing flaps uselessly from its elytra casing. Antennae droop and bend at odd angles. Tibia are missing. Pus oozes from lacerated segments.

In that broken state, N saw her through blurred vision. She comes upon him gently, though her bronze frons (or is it a face) glows with a fierce inner light. Her brown forelegs (or are they hands) wrap around his dented pronotum. Her tibial teeth (or are they fingers) intertwine with his. Her soft antennae (or are they eyelashes) nuzzle his broken mandible. Being held like this feels familiar to N even after the change. He knows her still. He knows, too, that she cannot be here for her scent is not with her. Yet here she is nursing him through the cold.

What has this world done to you?

Though the answer is clear, monstrously clear, she loves him still. Though this hard shell holds not a trace of her son, he is still her child to hold. And though the miles separate them, she knows instinctively to nurse him through this dark hour. With his last breath, N groans a sound like the first said four decades before.

Ma

Across the broken shell of this country, this United States, a nurse feels her son calling. Feels his cry in her bones. She reaches through the veil to tend him tenderly. Some bonds, it seems, transcend time and space and the most monstrous changes wrought upon us by history.

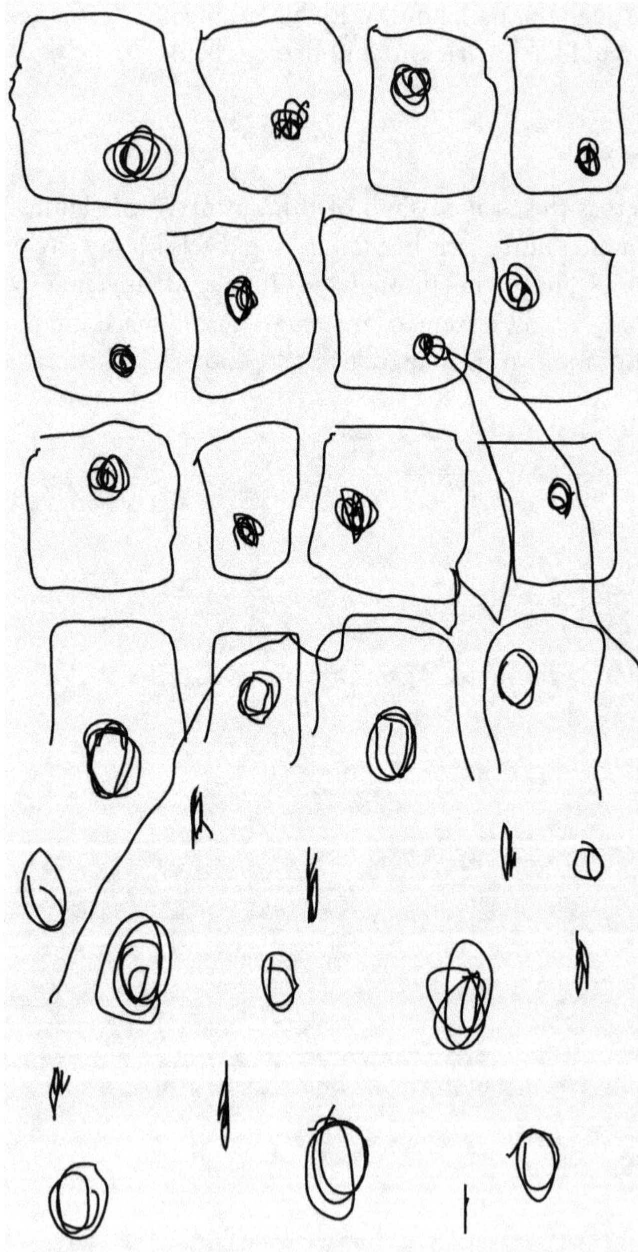

VI. Prometheus Unwired

Syme stood before the humanoid figure submerged in an embryonic tank. His augmented glasses saw through skin to the nanobots at work: Millions of little machines traced phosphorescent lines through veins and nerves as they rebuilt N with branded CRISPR tools and 3D printed silicon fibers, reprogrammed his mind with AI neural networks indistinguishable from the real thing. The body: a map; its lines pulsing and aglow.

Focusing on one line, Syme rode the data points inward to the microscopic terrain mapped by his nanobots, where he stood atop a recaptured cell like a captain aboard his flagship.

He saw war before him in real time. His nanobattalions decimated chitinous cells, speared them like giant kraken, split them open till they revealed a heavenly gate through which they poured to work miracles, to rebuild Jacob's Ladder so Gods could climb down among us. For Syme, this scene outdid any by Bosch, Blake, or Dante. And *this* was *his* creation, his paradise regained.

Taking a screen grab, Syme inserted a text note for his future memoirs:

AT THE INTERSTICES OF NEUROSCIENCE,
NANOTECH, AI AND SECURITY
THERE EXISTS A GOD.
AND, I AM HE!

I am He? I am Him? It is me? Eh, I'll return to it.

Inside the tank, the old spark of N was resurrected from data — from clusters of transactions and micro-transactions, from word searches and seemingly erased Google histories, from posts and emails that converged into cumulous word clouds, from photos and videos decoded to reveal mountains of history and the emotional vistas of a lifetime.

There were gaps, of course, but these were seamlessly filled by AI that knew N, knew the stars under which he was born, knew what gripped his awareness, what elicited emojis, what got his heart pounding and feet moving. Even in the absence of *his* data, the AI found N, a vacant little whirlpool shaped by the ocean of data collected from loved ones, friends and unfriends, those passed on streets and highways without a passing thought.

The tech had retrieved N's soul or, at least, its closest approximation.

As the embryonic fluid drained, N read the sensation of accumulated ones and zeroes that added up to a primal scream of terror and gratitude for being brought into

Being. He heard this scream not knowing what it was to scream. He heard it not knowing what it was to hear.

Syme smiled and, with a few twitches of his eye, sent a direct message to the chancellor, investors, and the silent partners that funded his research. The subject line:

IT IS DONE!

VII. Uncanny Valley

N woke to find himself an approximation of a human being or, as Syme would say, *augmented.*

He felt his neural networks booting up to unveil what his eyes saw: room, *my* room. Window, window of *my* room.

He looked out that window at the purple dawn. The accumulated data points fed through his system, fast as light, neural networks conversing with nanobots to conjure the appropriate electro-chemicals for {curiosity} which, in turn, relayed back to the mind the following:

Why is the sky the color purple?

Not expecting an answer, his system felt {surprise} to hear his own voice answer with an elegant explanation: *The sky can appear purple for a number of reasons, including: optical illusion, scattering of light, volcanic aerosols, thinning clouds.*

N's system accounted for curiosity and surprise, allowed them, factored them into functionality, then dialed them down. Functionality was priority now. His old data sets had established a well-worn vector that would serve that function: Wake, check email and social media, bathroom, coffee and scroll, run, shower, coffee and scroll, teach, eat and scroll, grade, stream and scroll, sleep.

He checked his phone. Amid junk mail was the chancellor's systemwide condolence about the English director and a message from his union. The latter, flagged as urgent, requested member votes on a systemwide strike. None of it processed through the brain-fog that appeared with that message. The words were there, but they were like spent cartridges stumbled upon in the dark. That phrase actually came to his mind: *spent cartridges.* It meant something to N. Something right there. But he couldn't reach it through the fog. He deleted the email and brewed his coffee, hoping it would lift the fog.

Looking out the window again, he saw purple had given way to blue. *Clear skies with a high of 72°.* He knew finer details, too — the precipitation, wind, humidity, and upon hearing the Pacific he knew the surf report — but all this was extraneous to the vector. The fog lifted, and he saw his path clearly mapped.

* * *

On his way to class, N passed a grassy knoll adjacent to the main thoroughfare that led to the futurist library.

N paused there, for reasons he couldn't know. He stared blankly at several students lazing on newly installed hammocks. He read a sign, staked in the grass, that warned against "discrimination" and "illegal camping."

A nearby commotion pulled N's attention back to the walkway where he saw an older man, red with rage, shouting at two students. The students, faces concealed behind keffiyehs, stood stone silent. One held a sign that read "Never Again Not for Anyone." The other wore a patch with a rainbow circled by doves.

N saw the man turning from the latter to the former like a bull caught between two red capes.

Do you know what they do to people like you in Palestine! And you! How can you betray your people!

He pulled out his iPhone, aimed it at the students, as if it were loaded.

Cowards! You can't even show your faces!

The students remained unphased as the man circled them with his phone. N could see the livestream filtering across the ether, angry emojis mirroring the man's face. The students only moved when they spotted campus police orbiting. They took this as signal and vanished into the crowd of onlookers and passersby. Seeing them disappear, the man's rage turned to the policeman, steamed for a minute, before finally retreating inwards where it ate away at his innards.

N tried to process this scene. Silicon synapses fired as he analyzed the man's words, the slogan, the patch. Seeking the truth of these things, all he got was a flood of information indistinguishable from disinformation, facts mixed with alternative facts. He tried to push through, to the other side of this torrent, felt himself approaching data sets of people who heard the drone's whir, who felt the fire and rubble. Close. So close. Then, nothing. Blank. And in that blank, he asked a desperate question:

What do I think of this war?

Nothing.

Synapses fired again, revising the question to one his AI could manage:

What does a Leftist think of this War?

Laid out before him, in his mind's eye, was a multitude of contradictory perspectives, arranged encyclopedically like a wiki then, in a flash, assembled as corridors in a virtual library. He could travel down any of those corridors, if curiosity called him, but curiosity conflicted with functionality and, since that was his prime directive, blankness was best.

Before giving himself over, N felt goosebumps rise on his nape, a visceral warning from the last rogue chitinous cells. The feeling passed as these cells were detected and put down by nanobots that moved, as drones move, over conquered territory.

*   *   *

For the next few months, N stayed in his lane. He woke (without regarding the purple sky), checked email and social media, went to the bathroom, drank coffee and scrolled, ran, showered, drank more coffee and scrolled, taught, ate and scrolled, graded, streamed and scrolled, slept, woke and repeated.

The familiar groove only shifted as new data entered his field. A protest here. Preachers there. A new billboard displaying an academic celebrity: Gerhard Syme, Dual Nobel Recipient & CEO of General AI.

N scanned this billboard and his mind output what needed to be known

Professor Emeritus Gerhard Syme breaks ground at the interstices of neuroscience, nanotech, AI and security. His recent research led to the foundation of General AI, a subsidiary of General Atomics. Dr. Syme was this year's double Nobel recipient in Science and Peace for his pathfinding work that is decreasing recidivism rates in California prisons.

N saw, behind closed eyes, a streaming record of Syme's research. Four feral rats first tore and clawed at each other. When injected with Syme's patented nanotech PaxMachina®, the four worked together to solve an intricate puzzle. It was vivid, this technicolor waking dream of gnashing teeth and squeaks of pain, giving way to the silent motion of four rats as one. What was not so clear was Syme's prison research. It only existed as an impenetrable data cloud. N could only trace the contours of that shape without ever getting inside.

Banking this data, N returned to his route. That route continued day after day, month after month.

To look at N during this time was to see a man doing better than ever. He was fitter and calmer. Always smiling. He was nimbler in the classroom, too, having developed a knack for defusing tension and getting derailed conversations back on track.

A sampling of N's course evaluations from this period corroborate that he was, in fact, at the top of his game:

His class is a pleasant escape from all the tension… he's so nice… he deepens our understanding of the world by showing us all sides… he shows us how to join conversations with a fair and balanced voice…the only complaint I have about the course is that it must end!

By far the greatest marker of N's achievement was the Chancellor's Award for Teaching Excellence. No teacher, N was told, had received so many nominations. The chancellor, it should be noted, was not present at the ceremony.

* * *

Life went smoothly until two unexpected data clouds floated into N's sensory field. The first, a call from his sister, came on like a thunderhead. He heard the storm brewing in her voice.

— Hey, N. Do you have a sec?

— Yes. I have a few minutes before teaching.

— Thanks. I don't know… I don't know what to do anymore.

He's not sending money. He told me I've got to get a job. But the kids. I'm doing everything I can for them…

N felt her words as a hard rain of ones and zeroes that he followed to her cloud. Looking in, he saw empty bank accounts, unpaid bills, half-completed MediCal and CalFresh e-forms, toxic text exchanges between her and her ex-husband.

— *I've got nothing left by the time I get the kids to school. Today, I tried opening my résumé. But all I saw were the gaps. It's like I haven't existed for a decade. I just shut down and went back to bed for an hour. I'm sorry. I know you're busy.*

— *I have time. Class doesn't start for a few minutes.*

— *Thanks. He came back again last month. I didn't tell you. So stupid! Fell for it again. He was good for a week, just like he used to be, but then he was pulled back to his work, back to the screen. It's like that damn company, General AI, has tentacles. It pulls him in every time, changes him. He was here but not here. When he wasn't looking at the screen, he was hollow. There was nothing in his eyes. When I tried to pull him back, the rage returned.*

Pulling from his reconstituted silicon memory, N configured a question which, he noticed, was harder to articulate than other thoughts.

— *Did he do it again?*

Silence but N felt the cumulous cloud of his sister hovering.

— Yes. But that's it. No more. I threw him out. When he was leaving, he yelled the worst things at me, called me a worthless piece of shit. Right in front of the kids. And now he doesn't send us a dime. All I have is what ma sends, but you know how I feel about that. She's seventy-six. She should be retired. What can I do? Maybe he's right. I am worthless.

Confronted with the final statement, N entered transactional mode. He examined his bank account to see what he could send her, but his algorithm told him this would not calm the storm. In a single blink, he extended his search over data oceans, past continents of practical solutions that would only cause more stress, finally coming to a small island in the stream. Though flagged as a "site of potential propaganda," N landed on the island. As he did, he understood it held the corpus of Marxist feminist writers, one of whom currently rose up as a digital ghost extending her hand to N.

N beheld her face. A face like Dreyer's Joan of Arc, beatific, only this warrior saint was older and Italian as was clear in her sweet *benvenuta*. As their digital fingers met, N felt a new feeling {communion} and, suddenly, he had words for his sister.

— You are not worthless. Your labors with those kids are essential to society. They are its future. Your labors at home allowed their father to labor. You fed him, you cleaned, did laundry, managed budgets, were expected to please him. He fed on your labor. The company that fed on him fed on your labor. The markets to which that company is bound fed on your labor. No, you are not worthless. The

fact that this society has devalued your labor doesn't make that any less true. You are its foundation. Most don't see that. But I see.

Rather than easing the storm, these words opened it. She cried a wounded cry that washed over them both and left N with a thought that *this*, this shared feeling uncanny in itself, is life.

— It'll be okay.

— I hope so.

N's stomach turned as he ended the call. He had crossed a line that could no longer be crossed. Some force behind his algorithm would ensure that. Closing his eyes, he saw the island sinking until it disappeared, not just for him, but for all future augmented travelers. A single act of trespass had eradicated a lineage from the metaverse.

His ill feelings subsided as nanobots did their work, rebalanced chemicals and shut down restricted neural networks, so that he could get on task. He was "good" again. He taught, ate and scrolled, graded, streamed and scrolled, slept, woke and began again.

The only time his awareness leapt to the surface was passing the banner of Dr. Syme on Library Walk. He felt it pulling at him, as if by magnetism, that quickly reversed to push him back to on track.

* * *

The second cloud came to N carrying ill winds that shot, like little arrows, through his smart phone.

— Hello, mister. I haven't heard from you. Everything okay?

His ma's voice—he hears something new within it, a foreboding rasp of lungs, that he knows she will not tell him about.

He rides the miasmic sound into her data cloud and sees the scans: the little fibrous lesions that spread even now as they spoke. His ghostly fingers work over them, stupidly trying to swipe them away. He processes the doctor's notes, cross-references medical data, analyzes asbestos lawsuits against the hospitals, runs algorithms to determine her time left, flags flights he can afford in the allotted time.

As he does so, he notices her cloud is tethered to others that form a blood red data storm of companies extracting her monthly payments, companies betting on and against her life, companies that will feed on the vapors of her even after death. He speaks, now, as his avatar moves through virtual space.

— I'm okay, ma. How are you?

— Tired. But okay. They've been giving me more patients. And can you believe, they started monitoring us with cameras to make sure we don't take a break!

He is pulled to silent grainy surveillance footage of ma after she completed rounds on her fifth nightshift. Her coworker silently assures her she's got it from here. Ma's whole body sighs as she sits. With staggered breath, she lays her head down on the unadorned desk and begins to doze. N zooms in on her weary face, notes the wrinkles, those markers of six decades of caring labor, six decades of pouring her energy into maintaining life, six decades spent so she could keep her children afloat only to see that, in the end, she cannot.

Her voice pulls him back to the here and now.

— *There are more and more patients coming in, addicted to new street drugs. They have this vacant sad look, poor things. And the new nurses don't know what to do! They've been pushed through the system. They just feed data into charts. No time to talk or even look at the patients. Then, the doctor's send out the same virtual scripts every time: PaxMachina. Well, I know they're getting wined and dined to write those scripts. And the patients who take it — you should see them! They leave with this smile on their face. But there's something behind it. Something worse than the vacant look they came in with. They want us to believe that drug is a miracle. Hmph! I wasn't born yesterday, N.*

N saw the cloud of data that was her hospital, saw its electric tentacles connected like a dread umbilical to ma's cloud. He watched it siphoning energy from her and the other clouds of caring laborers and patient debtors. It grew larger, more luminous, as they shrank and greyed. But he saw too that the hospital was caught in the snare of larger tentacles, one of which led to General AI. That tentacle undulated as if taunting him. But beyond that, so far beyond it could have been mistaken as the background, the ghastly outline of a dark mountainous shape that fed upon all the siphoned energy. Ignoring that Thing for now, N returned to her.

— I remember you'd say that when I was a kid. I'd lift your eyelids as you slept, ask for money for basketball cards. You'd grunt just so I let go. When you woke, you'd find five dollars missing. I'd deny it. And then you'd say…

— I wasn't born yesterday.

She laughs and, for a moment, cannot push down the cough. The full sound of it allows N to finish processing her timeline. He sees he only has time and money enough to make it back to her once more. That's it. His mind begins auto-generating text before his eyes. Words cobble together from synthesized memories, words he would need to deliver to those who'll mourn. But the feeling that comes from these words is too intense. He doesn't catch thought slipping into speech.

— Stop!

— Are you okay, N?

— Sorry. There's just something going on. I want it to stop. But I can't make it.

— I'm sorry, N. Is it Gaza? I heard about the encampments. Terrible. Calling riot police. I thought this was America. But remember, you can only take on so much, N. Take care of yourself. I'll send money.

*— It's okay, ma. I'm okay. I don't need money. You take
care of yourself. Get some rest. And don't worry about
the cameras. I bet you they're not even recording. Just a
scare tactic.*

As he says it, N reaches his avataric hand through virtual
space to hack the cameras so that ma will be forever
awake, alert, even as she dozes off on her unadorned desk.

*— I'll try. Check your bank account later. The money should
have gone through. Love you, mister.*

N sees $200 crossing digital space, wired from her
account to his, and his body strangely comprehends this,
not as a transaction, but as an embrace.

— I love you.

N sits in silence for a moment. He feels nanobots doing
their work to restore balance, to give him the same vacant
smile as ma's patients. He scratches his arms, tears at his
chest, hopelessly claws against the little drones inside his
body. Before euphoria sets in, he takes out an old photo
tucked in his journal before all the changes. A remnant
from the analog age, the image is faded now, sunkissed
and golden.

There she is, ma, frozen in amber. He sees her, fresh-
faced, holding him as a toddler. Those hands holding
him. Those hands that worked their way out of a barrio,
that did their caring work for six decades, that soon won't
be able to care for anyone, not even herself, that on the
appointed day {plus or minus two} will turn to dust.

Closing his eyes, his silicon mind conjures memory. He is in that photo, in its approximation, looking up at her airbrushed face through a false metallic glow akin to a Disney movie. He cycles through all available filters but nothing comes close to the aura of analog. Residing there, in her arms, he notices her hands twisting like tentacles around him. They are *not* her hands. This is not *her*, this polished simulacrum. And he. He is *not* who was held.

He opens his eyes to the photo. It has become a talisman, a totem, that his AI cannot integrate. As nanobots push him towards a dopamine high, curve his lips to a false smile, the photo pulls him toward melancholy. Resting in this sensation, as if under a dark angel's wing, he knows. Knows where he must go to wake from this nightmare.

PAX

VIII. Contracted,
or, The Insect Who Came in From the Cold

The marine layer settled over Torrey Pines, gray and thick, but N did not need its shroud to pass like a spook through the security of General AI.

Circling the eco-brutalist campus, he moved as a shadow against vined walls. He easily timed his movements to avoid the guards who he saw as data clouds floating in and around the building. When he reached locked doors, he simply waved one hand to give the receiver what it needed to slide open, waved the other to relay looped footage to cameras.

Inside, he moved swiftly from floor to floor. He could feel himself get closer to the place he was meant to be. It was as if that place held a homing beacon that caused his pulse to quicken, reaching its peak when he came to the double doors of Dr. Syme's office.

The doors slid open into a two-room suite bigger than N's apartment. The main room was dimly lit and vacant, while its adjoining room appeared, through a sliver of glass, dark and uninhabited.

He moved into the main room. It was minimalist in its arrangement: a gun-metal black desk with an open laptop that gave the room its artificial glow.

Faced with the laptop's biometric lock, N reshaped his eye to Syme's shape, mimicked perfectly the silver shards of iris, the black hole of pupil, the unique signature of retinal blood vessels. He was in.

He didn't have to dig deep to find the contracts that told the story of General AI. The tale was clear in charts, Excel sheets, and emails that showed how the corporation's reach extended into the Heartland of America, from the Rust Belt to the tar sands of Canada, from the coastal metropoles to the rubble of Gaza.

He read the corporate contracts. Scrolling through their numbers, he followed the data trails in his mind's eye. Taking shape from the clouds of data were warehouse workers and meatpackers, frackers and electric carmakers, gigworkers and caregivers with the same vacant smile his Ma saw in the hospital. He saw those on the other end of their labor smiling as they opened boxes, bit into burgers, drove Cybertrucks and Civics, swallowed the pill promising peace.

He clicked through to military contracts. He saw how the army had ordered a special brand of PaxMachina for its rebooted Human Terrain System. This new insight allowed him to enter hidden data clouds. N saw augmented anthropologists blending into tribal meetings, community meetings, and religious gatherings. These spooks knew exactly the right word or gesture to gain trust. He saw one sitting in a circle of elders. As he sat, sipping his tea, he flagged the elders for "suspect ideologies," scanned their biometrics, uploaded their imprints to the military's private metaverse where they would be tracked and legible for the duration of their lives.

N moved on.

Scanning Syme's inbox, he came to an e-mail with the subject line "The Question of Palestine Answered." The message, addressed to Pentagon and Israeli officials and blind copied to investors, promised a "gentle way" of ending the conflict. As Syme wrote, *The Palestinian question will be solved because, once treated with Pax-Machina, there will be no more Palestinians. It will make them human. Wholly human.*

But, as N saw in another email to top brass, the gentle way was a pipedream. Other contracts showed the immediate promise. Augmented old school warfare. N saw soldiers given megadoses that turned them into human war-machines fully integrated with their machineguns, drones, and bombs. He saw one flying a fleet of drones without any view screen. It looked as if she was performing tai chi, moving her body gracefully through space, each hand stroke a barrage of bombs. For a moment he saw what she saw. The horror. The horror become a video game.

This was enough for N. He felt sick, then immediately the sweet relief of PaxMachina flowing through his blood. He looked again at his photo to return to unease.

N had seen enough. As he retreated, he noticed the suite's other room had opened. His breath froze.

There, seated in the dark, Syme reclined corpselike. Behind his dark glasses, his eyes were unfocused and unblinking. N checked to see if Syme was breathing, no sign, then put hand to neck to feel for a pulse. That touch. It was like pressing an invisible button that catapulted N inward, into the 3D landscape mapped by nanomachines droning through his body.

* * *

— Where am I?

— The kingdom of your third eye. Our pineal fortress. Look now upon my wonders and find hope.

Syme and N's digital avatars stood upon a rampart, staring out at a sea of electric light. Within that sea, half submerged in its current, was the metallic sphere upon which the rampart was carved like a smirk, a logo. Above nanobots swarmed in patterns of hidden meaning.

— Why am I here?

— I have an affinity for you. You were the first. I rode you since your beginning. Or rather, I steered you. Do you think you came to me on your own accord? Do you think you were gifted enough to move as you have moved? I have been with you. Guiding you. Closing doors. Opening doors. Sure, I gave you room to play at being human, let you believe you were close to the real, let you feel deep emotions, face existential dread. But, in the end, it was

all very controlled. My little experiment. Just like the little rats in a maze who think they discover routes I program into their DNA.

– Why?

– I always wanted a child. And do you know the best gift you can give your child?

– What?

– Security masked in the illusion of freedom.

– So why bring me here?

– Out of love, my son. I want to share the bounty of our work. Without you, we wouldn't be on the verge of a final absolute peace. That goes for this inner kingdom and the outer. I wanted to share this peace with you. This peace of the Gods. Really share it. To do that, I'll give up that useless flesh bag you saw outside. It still has life, but not life like yours, not the life of the Alpha reaching toward the Omega. I will be your eternal passenger, witnessing, as you take your inheritance and claim our birthright. That is our final choice.

– And if I say no?

– No use. Your algorithm has already been set. Our choice has already been made. All of this is a mere kindness.

– No.

On cue, the nanoswarms freeze above the pineal fortress. Each bot vibrates wildly, as if something is trapped inside, something that wants out. It breaks free in a vomit of black chitinous tentacles. Writhing, the unleashed grotesqueries fall like black rain. They slither and grope, slide and pulsate across the metallic sphere, tear through its metal skin to reveal a single cyclopean eye, onyx and terrible.

Elsewhere across the whole inner landscape of N, silicon cells follow suit, rip open, release chitin that has taken on the cybernetic character of its host.

Syme's avatar screams in pain. He feels, in the outer world, the creature's pincers digging into his face and pressing glasses deep into flesh. There is no way out now. He then tastes the acidic liquid, salivating from the creature's mouth into his, carrying a viral load of chitinous nanomachines into his body.

He looks to where N had stood on the ramparts. Nobody there. All that remains, a photo. A mother and her child, perfect except for her fingers.

* * *

Syme knows there is no exit, no way back to his physical body. Even now, his consciousness within the beast, he can feel it awaiting his next move.

His avatar sees one doorway and takes it.

He is inside his own body now, ensnared in tentacles

neither fully synthetic nor fully organic. Looking out, he sees the host of hijacked nanobots. They swarm into hieroglyphs, sigils, sacred geometries. There is no algorithm here, only anarchy. When they tire, they turn to their host. Tentacles latch onto Syme's cells like giant kraken engulfing ships. For a moment, Syme expects these creatures to bond, as his nanobots did with N, but instead they tear the vessels apart. They feast.

Terrorists!

* * *

N stands next to the puddle that was Syme. Nothing usable in the waste, so he moves to the outer room. Facial feelers caress the surface till they find an input. Plugged in, he scans for the data he needs. He has it. Has the Thing's scent, knows where Its arms are found. There, buried in silos. There, in nondescript factories. There, in unmarked warehouses. He knows the coordinates, sees the vectors leading there. Before unplugging, N uploads a viral load that moves across the web, reaches the cloud of General AI, tears and rends till there isn't a trace.

Outside the building, a guard sneaks a smoke, sees the creature moving through Torrey Pine mist like a locomotive bound… bound for what? For glory? Infamy? None of that matters now. There is only the scent, the pull, and destiny written in the dark.

Interlude 2. Fire Eater

In another time, long after the Great Solar Flare, the penultimate chapter of N's life had become legend. The tale of Fire Eater, it was called, and the scops who sang it sung of a holy beast that stalked the old empire. Droning in low tones, they crouch low and lower still, sniff the ground to mimic the beast as it followed the scent to empire's hidden caves. In and off the moors, it came, moving relentlessly. It could not be stopped by the imperial guard who the scops pantomime with sticks that seem to shoot fire. The beast cut through all these flimsy defenses, they sing, till it found what it hungered for. Fire chalices. When the scops reach this point in the tale, they gesture wildly to show the way the beast devoured the fire. They gesture at swallowing, crouch inward holding their tummies, then make themselves tall and wide to show how the beast's stomach reversed the old magical spell. $E=mc^2$. They sing of how the beast grew as it fed, how its dark mass absorbed the force of fire held in each chalice. It grew. It grew. It grew. Droning on in a tongue yet to come, the scops slouch toward the sunrise mirroring the movements of the beast as it made for its final destination. The children, snug in their parents' arms, giggle at the farfetched thought of world ending fires.

Above them the planes appear, dropping snow gathered from the north to cool the midsummer play. And across vast distances, networked now by kinship rather than wire, other scops sing of those that ate fire.

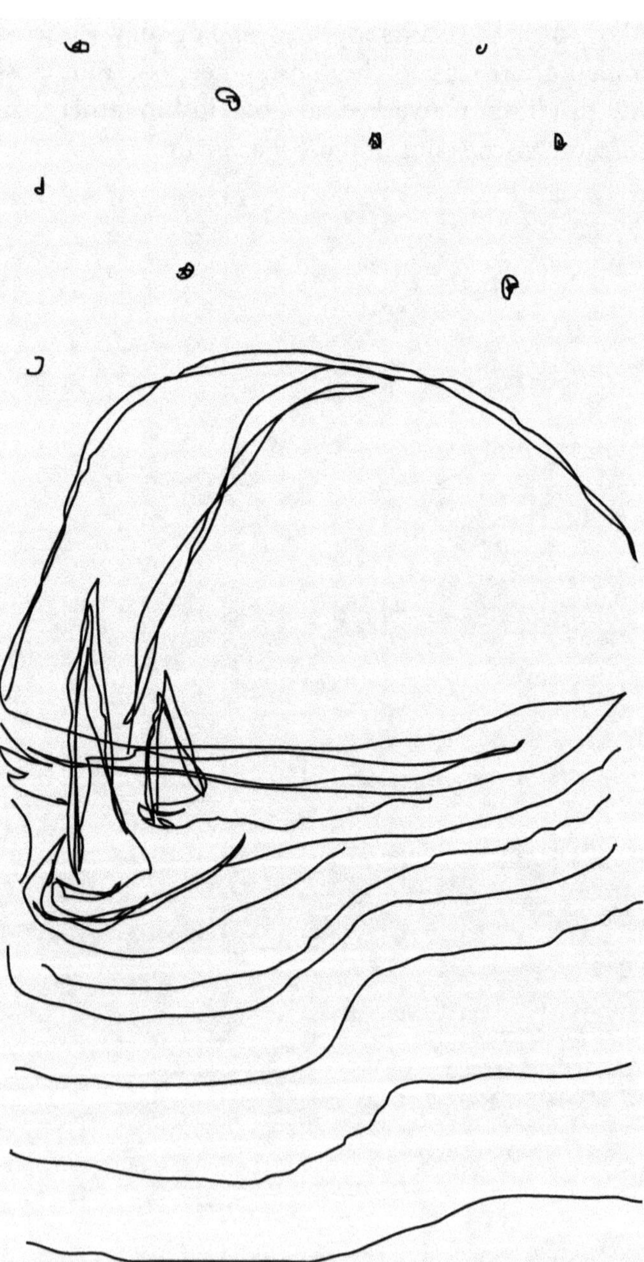

IX. Slouching Toward Bethlehem

The eyes of the world are on the monster, larger than Everest now, as it lumbers into the Atlantic.

A string of Apache helicopters follow like gnats trailing an elephant. For weeks, they tried their weapons, but every bomb was subsumed into its dark mass. Finally, a cease fire had been called. That declaration hid the fact that whatever stockpiles had not been eaten by the monster were now spent. The silos were empty. The warehouses and factories were ruins. Still, the gnats follow in futile procession.

From the penthouses and skyscrapers of Manhattan, the influencers, movers, disruptors look out while sipping champagne. From his golden tower, the president-to-be turns his back, jealous of the monster's unbridled power.

In Midtown, N's ma looks up from her charts to see the monster's progress on a patient's television. She is pulled back by a code blue. Her next minutes are spent intubating a man that the young nurses and doctors were at a loss to save. She ignores her own labored breath as she walks to her office. Alone at her desk, she joins thousands of essential workers across the city who balance their labor with the livestream.

On Liberty Island, a mix of protestors, worshippers, and reporters gather to watch the monster's departure. It takes hours. Most tire and make for the ferries. But some remain, eyes fixed on the black mountainous shell receding into the horizon. One amongst them prays to Christ for some sign that the Father sent this beast. Another, a devotee of Mother Kali, recites a mantra that speaks of a violent end to this violent yuga. A child, part of the indigenous contingent, mouths *Turtle Island*. But most look on in wordless awe as this small black sun on the wrong horizon recedes to a point and is gone.

* * *

A cease fire had been called on the creature but not on Palestine. The last remaining stockpiles still fall. The living and the dead remain under the rubble. The creature can sense them as it looks down on the Holy Land. It pauses, there, in the warm waters off the coast, its huge wake ebbing against the ruined coastline. Still as death it looms. Some who watch think it might just stay there, an inert volcano.

* * *

Inside the beast, within the onyx orb once a pineal gland, a ghostly passenger bears witness to the end.

N sees his mountainous being make landfall. He sees a child throwing a stone at heaven. Hears a sniper's jaw clench as he takes aim at the child even though the apocalypse is in full view. Sees the armies launch their final ballistics. Sees drone operators hopelessly gesturing in far-off rooms. Feels the force of 2000-pound bombs imploding against his exoskeleton and being subsumed into more of his dark mass. Hears people cry, curse, pray, fall silent.

For Gaza, a normal day.

Then N sees the beast begin its instinctual work. Its great claws, the size of skyscrapers, churn the land and people, crush buildings, wipe away barbed wire walls and demolish whole settlements. It rolls the land in upon itself, unearths corpses not seen for decades and soil not seen since Christ and Muhammad walked the earth. This wreck, this humus of existence, is rolled into a massive ball that looms larger as the beast lurches forward, looms larger as creature-and-ball take on a centripetal force of their own, a mass that rolls onward with the force of uncategorizable storms, rolls onward through the Holy Land from Gaza to Jerusalem, through Syria and Iraq, Iran and Afghanistan, India, China, Japan, across the sea where it makes landfall in San Diego. Nothing can be done to stop its motion. Kinetic energy sparks lightning storms, whips up whirlwinds, churns tsunamis. The beast and its ball exert a gravitational pull. Everything is pulled into its gyre: highways, cities, forests. Its hunger is insatiable. Its vectors set. It keeps spinning, spinning, spinning across the globe until all is consumed in its dark mass.

After a century, when the last prayers fall silent, the

monster knows its work is done. It feels, inside the dung ball, seeds stirring. They claw forth in a starburst, these children of a new age, lurch toward their creator who sees fire through translucent skin. They nuzzle into its fleshy underside, consume with a hungry love.

Finally, peace.

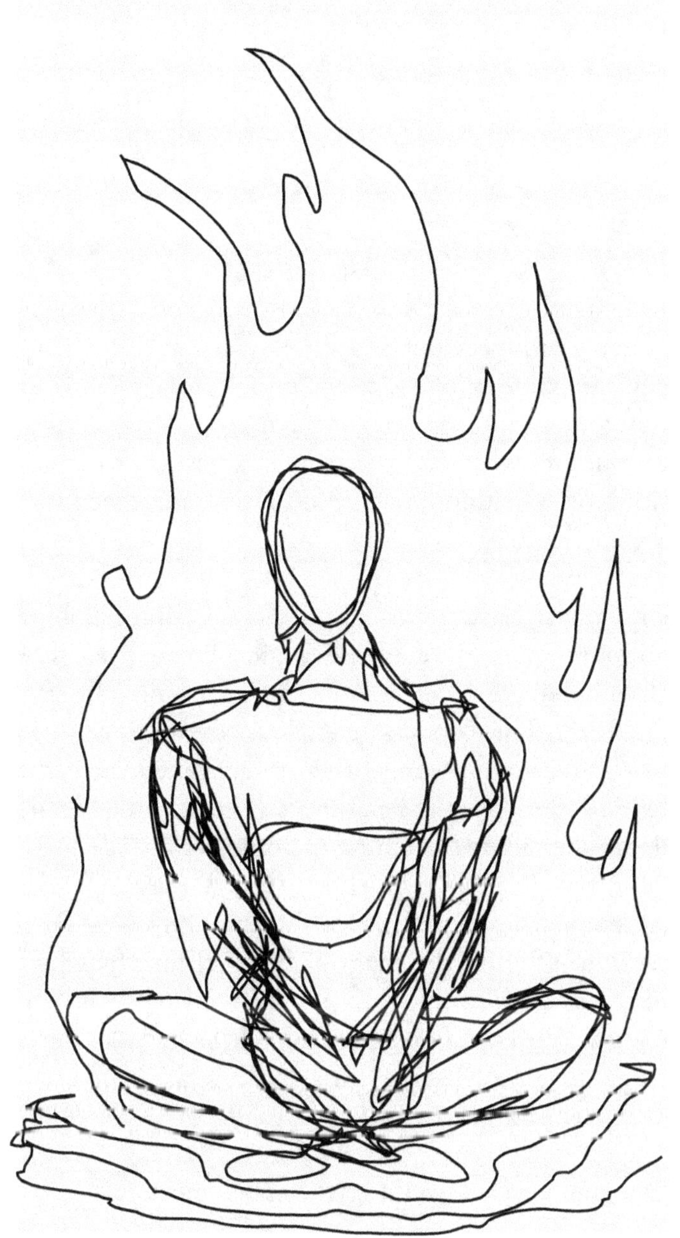

X. Incomplicity

What is prophecy but a reading of an algorithm to its end? Machines prophesize when they predict the likely outcome of a given data set. An animal, say a frog, prophesizes when it predicts precisely where the algorithm of fly-within-air will end so its tongue meets it at the fateful point.

The monster, this mountain of silicon-chitin, had the gift of prophecy. Its data set was all encompassing. The child holding his rock and the sniper clenching his jaw. Pure data. The drip of a general's coffee machine as he adjusts his tie in the mirror. Pure data. The itch on the fighter pilot's scalp as he awaits a general's orders. Pure data. The billions watching the monster livestreamed. Pure data. The billions unable to watch. Pure data. The ecosystems enmeshing them all, from the tiniest fluctuations of air to the beat of a billion butterfly wings to the unseen undulations of a billion times a billion worms. Pure data. This web of life. The manmade matrix enmeshing it. All fed into the algorithm that N had read to its terminal point.

One step forward would set the ball in motion.

But a sound gives N pause. A child screams for her mama. She wants to be held and cannot be held. She wants to move and cannot move.

All abstractions of the future are wiped away by the child's scream. It is concrete. No. It is flesh and blood and air surrounded by concrete. N knows, just hearing it, that the child is held together by the rubble. Move it and she ceases to be. Leave her and she ceases to be.

The cry goes silent.

N considers again the algorithm he witnessed play till the end. If he moves an inch, it will come to be. Yet he knows, if he moves that inch, what he will become:

The Thing this child feels bearing down upon her grave. The Thing all martyrs see in their final moments. The Thing he felt stalking the shadows. He can smell It now, smell that Thing he has chased, inside himself.

A final cry from the rubble.

For N, all turns dark, as if his whole being winks. In the darkness, he sees a faint flame growing brighter like someone is moving toward him with a candle.

N sees him now. The burning man in his lotus posture. He still mouths the names. Tonight, he will mouth more: The child and her mother who lies in the make-shift UNRWA hospital. Their names will be written in flame. And N's name. Some, who have the eyes to see, will see their names flick up across the dark of Revelle

Plaza, the emblazoned letters flowing continuously into each other, endlessly repeated until war's end.

The little ghost inside the monster gives a final command to the monstrous particles of its being.

The center should not hold.

The eyes of the world are on the dung beetle as it dissolves. *Just look at that, it's dead; it's done for,* one says to another as they clink glasses and see their stocks rebound. But their eyes don't see how its dust carries across the rubble, how it blows in four directions, how the wind carries atoms to those in the midst of the same monstrous and beautiful change. Fire eaters waiting death. Fire eaters waiting to be reborn from this shit. They consume his pieces till the monster becomes their own.

Coda. Sunny Day

The strand of Rockaway Beach, NY was mostly vacant save for one family: N's ma, her daughter and her four grandchildren.

The health officials had said to stay indoors, for fear of what was carried on the wind, but they hadn't listened. Ma hated the beach, hated the sand she had to sweep, but today she wanted to be there with her grandkids. It was the first time they'd been given their father's permission to travel back East with their mother.

So, ma's daughter and grandkids wheeled her to the beach as she held the baby in her arms. She got exhausted walking these days, breathing was a struggle, but she made the final stretch on foot.

They set up their blanket just outside the sweep of high tide. Ma's daughter watched her twins play in the surf. They hadn't a care in the world. She hoped that would last. Her eldest boy took a seat in the lotus posture, his back to his mother and grandma. He'd become dour in the last few years. She didn't know what was in his mind as he looked eastward beyond the horizon. Turning to ma, she saw her bronze face glowing as she held the baby. Reaching instinctively for her phone, she felt it not there, so she took the picture in her mind.

As she did, she heard the twins scream…

Look!

They all face the sky. The sun lights the chitinous dust, causing it to sparkle like glitter, a mirror image of the million sundrops on the ocean. This dust rains down on them, a soft sparkling rain. Ma takes a deep breath in, deeper than in years, and she begins to heal.

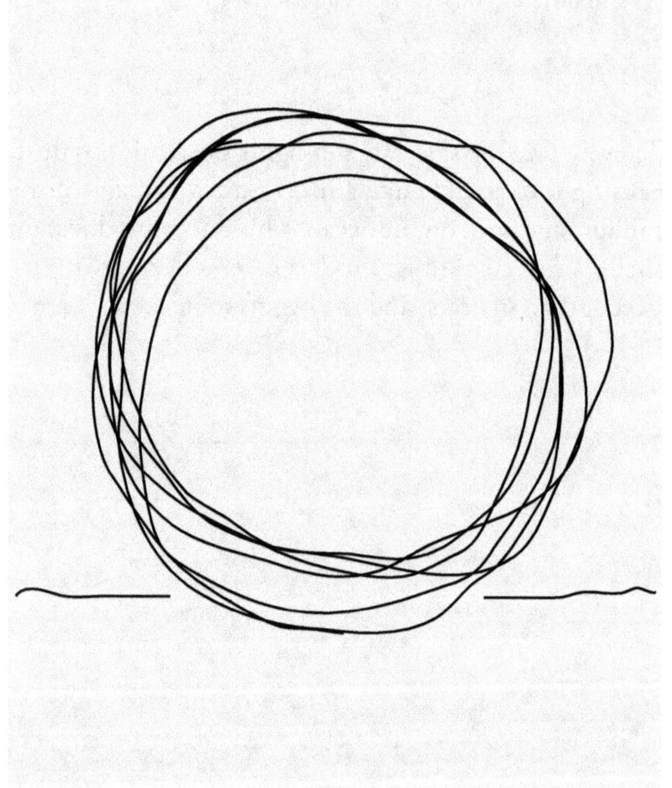

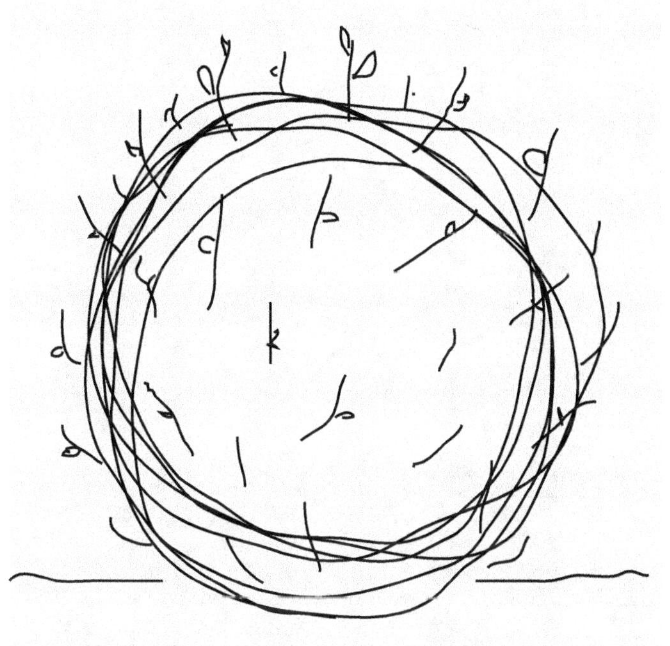